FIRST Child

Written by Jen Nicolazzo

Illustrations by Kinga Martin

For my amazing kids, Will and Hayden, who are my everyday inspiration, and to Norm my first child who always acts like I just came home. A huge thanks to my husband Jon who never stops believing in me and my dreams, and to my mom, dad and sissy, who are my biggest cheerleaders in life. To Jackie Blake's 2nd grade class who gave me great ideas for the book, and last but not least, to our sweet Betty who brought so much love and light to our lives.

We will never forget you!

Illustrations by Kinga Martin
Book Design by Kyla Korytoski

ISBN 978-1-7333263-0-8
Published by Nighthawk Creative, LLC
jen.nicolazzo@gmail.com

My life was amazing.

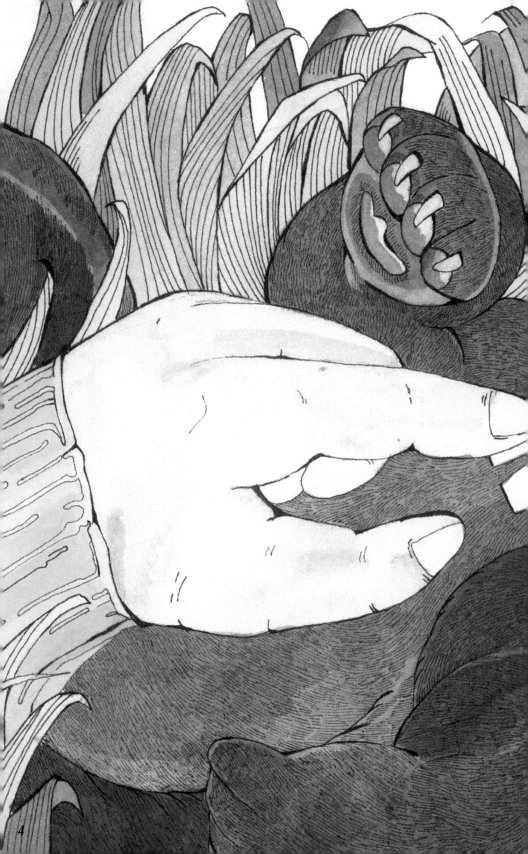

There was so much LOVE,

so many toys...

and sooo much couch time.

Then one rainy day I was looking out the window when I saw it. My mom and dad looked *SO* happy carrying something.

WHAT WAS IT?
A football? A newspaper?

No, wait, it MOVED!!!
Oh. My. Goodness.

My life was about to change. This cute
moving football was well... *so cute!*

He was so *loved.*

He had so many toys!

And **W A Y** more
couch time than me.

But the football got older, and well
he started to like me. He even hugged
me with his whole body!

Life was good again ...

For about 2 years
and 9 months.

You GUESSED IT! Another Football.

This one was dressed in *a lot of pink*
and cried *a lot* more.

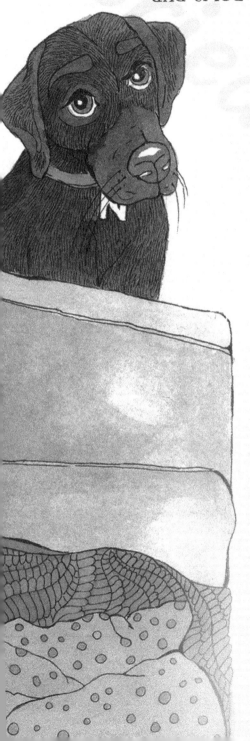

Life was moving fast,
and I felt like I was
mostly in the way.

But then this pink football grew up
and played with me too! Sometimes,
she even called me her *BESTIE!*

I was the man again...
It was the *COOLEST.*

Until... Oh no, not another football. But another one of MY KIND. This one was a girl. One with a past life...

with history.

They really liked her,
and she could do no wrong.

"Oh... Betty is sooo *CALM*."

"Oh... Betty is sooo *SWEET*."

"Oh... Betty is sooo *CUTE*"

Wait a minute!
WHAT AM I? *Chopped liver?*

Betty didn't even like the water...
and fetching? NOPE. Not once.

But me, I'm like the *Olympian* of ball fetchers.

Betty was special, and she knew it.
I guess it was nice having company
when the humans all left for the day.

I mean we weren't CUDDLING or anything...

It ended up working out in my favor.
She'd distract our dad human at
dinner and I would get all the dropped

Food Bits.

One day, I noticed Betty leave without me.
I waited...

and waited.

My humans came back a few hours later,
but no Betty. My family looked sad.
Was she GONE?
She seemed so tired and she had that limp.

I started to think it was all my fault.

I was back to getting all the love
and treats, but somehow I didn't feel better.

It was then that I realized that *MORE* family means you always have someone to curl up, ROMP and beg for food with.

I may be the *FIRST CHILD*, but I now know there's plenty of love to go around even when you have to share it.

I wonder how I'll share the love next?

Norm's extended family

37

CPSIA information can be obtained
at www.ICGtesting.com
Printed in the USA
BVHW022258211119
563784BV00007B/4/P